This book belongs to:

....

....

For my loves. - Jodie Parachini

To A.W.M. – Gill McLean

A NEW BURLINGTON BOOK
The Old Brewery
6 Blundell Street
London N7 9BH

Editor: Tasha Percy
Designer: Anna Lubecka
Editorial Director: Victoria Garrard
Art Director: Laura Roberts-Jensen

Copyright © QED Publishing 2014

First published in the UK in 2014 by QED Publishing
Part of The Quarto Group company

www.qed-publishing.co.uk

A catalogue record for this book is available from the British Library.

ISBN 978 1 78171 913 8

Printed in China

The Snake Who Said Shhh

Jodie Parachini   Gill McLean

NEW
BURLINGTON
BOOKS

The jungle was filled with noise on the day Seth was born.

Elephants trumpeted,

chimpanzees chattered...

Chi-keeee!

E-e-oo-oo

Squawk

Squawk

...and parrots squawked.

Seth slithered out of his leafy hole in the ground.
He stared, wide-eyed, at the trees
and loud animals around him.

Squeak

Mum nudged Seth's slippery body.
"Go on," she said. "Sssay sssomething."

Seth slurped the air with his tongue. Then he let out a big...

"shhhhhhh!"

"What did he say?"
the parrots squawked.

"You're supposed to say *hiss!*"
growled a grumpy leopard.

"Whoever heard of a snake with a lisp?"
cackled the chimpanzees.

Seth blushed.

"Don't lisssten to them, ssson," Mum said. "I think you sssound beautiful."

Seth tried again.

"**Shhhhhh**," he said.

The baboons fell about with laughter.

Seth slithered sadly back into his hole.

The jungle burst into a chorus of hoots and howls.

"Enough!" the leopard roared. "We must choose a gift for the new baby."

"How about a toothbrush for his fangs?" suggested a crocodile.

"No," the leopard said.
"An owl feather for his bed.
That's the present we always
give to a new baby snake."

"But I'm old," the owl hooted from his perch.
"I have no spare feathers left to give."

"A fresh leafy branch would be perfect for his nest," said the young bongo.

"Leaves are boring," the chimpanzees complained. "Let's catch him a nice tasty mouse!"

"What?" squeaked the dormouse.
"Let's throw him a party instead.
He can slither and dance and..."

"Snakes can't dance!"
called the sunbird.

The animals roared and squawked
and chirped and argued, each
yelling louder than the next.

They were so busy
squabbling that they
didn't notice the
little snake slide
out of his hole.

Grrr!

Snap!

Snap!

As he watched the fuss,
Seth grew sadder
and sadder.

At last, he'd had enough. Seth lifted his head as high as he could and shouted,

"SHHHHHHH!"

The jungle
fell silent.

"Maybe all he wants is some quiet," whispered the dormouse.

The animals looked at each other
and shrugged. No one spoke.
Then they stared at Seth.

Seth licked the air, then snuggled up with his Mum and smiled.

"Happy birthday, Seth," the animals whispered. The jungle was peaceful and still.

Next steps

Some snakes are dangerous and can be scary. Ask the children how they would feel if they came across a snake in the forest? Do Seth and his mother seem scary?

At first the other animals make fun of Seth for the way he talks. Ask the children if they have ever made fun of someone, or if anyone has made fun of them.

Ask the children whether they have ever tried to say a tongue twister. How does it make them feel if they can't say it, or if they can? Are there any words that they find difficult to say - like spaghetti, yellow or superstition?

Ask the children what kind of present they would take if they were going to a birthday party for a snake. Do they think silence is a good present? Would they like to receive silence as a present? Can they think of anyone else who might like peace and quiet as a present?

Are there times of the day when they like to be loud like the animals in the forest? Are there times when they prefer to be quiet?

Try acting out the story. Which roles are noisy and which are calm at the start? Does this change by the end?